Once Upon A Dream

Whispers In Verse

Edited By Lynsey Evans

First published in Great Britain in 2024 by:

Young Writers
Est. 1991

Young Writers
Remus House
Coltsfoot Drive
Peterborough
PE2 9BF
Telephone: 01733 890066
Website: www.youngwriters.co.uk

All Rights Reserved
Book Design by Ashley Janson
© Copyright Contributors 2024
Softback ISBN 978-1-83565-811-6
Printed and bound in the UK by BookPrintingUK
Website: www.bookprintinguk.com
YB0606U

FOREWORD

Welcome Reader, to a world of dreams.

For Young Writers' latest competition, we asked our writers to dig deep into their imagination and create a poem that paints a picture of what they dream of, whether it's a make-believe world full of wonder or their aspirations for the future.

The result is this collection of fantastic poetic verse that covers a whole host of different topics. Let your mind fly away with the fairies to explore the sweet joy of candy lands, join in with a game of fantasy football, or you may even catch a glimpse of a unicorn or another mythical creature. Beware though, because even dreamland has dark corners, so you may turn a page and walk into a nightmare!

Whereas the majority of our writers chose to stick to a free verse style, others gave themselves the challenge of other techniques such as acrostics and rhyming couplets. We also gave the writers the option to compose their ideas in a story, so watch out for those narrative pieces too!

Each piece in this collection shows the writers' dedication and imagination – we truly believe that seeing their work in print gives them a well-deserved boost of pride, and inspires them to keep writing, so we hope to see more of their work in the future!

CONTENTS

Independent Entrants

Tahlia (8)   1

Batley Parish CE Primary Academy, Batley

Ayesha Qadri (9)	2
Najeebah Mayat (9)	4
Isabella Walker (9)	5
Sanaa Sidat (9)	6
Asad Kamran (8)	7
Jamielee Glover (9)	8
Holly Cooke (9)	9
Muhammed Bin Anas (9)	10

Cuddington And Dinton CE School, Dinton

Amber Dyer (8)	11
Winnie Bernstein (8)	12
Amara Sewell (8)	14
Rosie Allen (7)	15
Aria Delnevo (7)	16
Eva Reng (7)	17
Amelie Smith (8)	18
Clara Wilby (8)	19
Vivienne Douglass (8)	20
Thea Andrew (8)	21
Henry Rush (8)	22
Christopher (7)	23
Josh Davis (8)	24

Fossebrook Primary School, Leicester

Daniel Ball (9)   25

Anarra Lakhani (9)	26
Freddie Dulon (8)	28
Lucas-James Gaskin Yurt (9)	29
Lewis Woodward (9)	30
Olly Marsden (9)	32
Riley Gledhill (9)	33
Sienna Farmer (8)	34
Julia Kilinska (8)	35
Emerson Vickers-Hunt (9)	36
Marysia Buk (9)	37
Jake Goodwin (8)	38
Spencer Williams (9)	40
Yashasvi Dadhich (9)	41
Ifeoluwa Alabi (9)	42
Aleksander Ryzner (9)	43
Jonah Goodwin (8)	44
Enrico Chauhan-Gerace (8)	45
Lucas Odedra (9)	46
Ava Stokes (9)	47
Johnpaul Shaju (9)	48
Thea Rodgers (9)	49
Oseana James-O'Callaghan (9)	50

Holy Cross Catholic Primary School, Liverpool

Nozinhle Nyoni (9)	51
Sasha Mswelanto (8)	52
Willow-Rose Fearns (9)	54

Le Cateau Community Primary School, Catterick Garrison

Ellie Moore (11)	55
Lily Robinson (11)	56
Hope Eveson (11)	57

Provost Williams CofE Primary School, Coventry

Ella Hands (9)	58
Sienna Gardner (9)	60
Joey Mcgovern (9)	62
Elizabeth Tasker (9)	63
Oakley Cox (9)	64
Sophie Dudley (9)	66
Musaad Saiyed (9)	67
Oscar Maunder (9)	68
Lewis Young (8)	69

St Eanswythe's CE Primary School, Folkestone

Rachel Moulder (11)	70
Pixie Faulkner (11)	71
Autumn McCairn (11)	72
Keira Murphy (11)	73

St Francis Primary School, Lurgan

Leo Hegarty (10)	74
Luca Goddard (10)	76
Emma Cullen (10)	77
Grace McAnarney (10)	78
Lily Jane Monaghan (10)	79
Sofia Murray (10)	80

St Mark's Primary School, Hanwell

Chloe Ross (10)	81
Elena Uzunska (9)	82
Charlie Melville-Smith (9)	83
Noah Sterritt (8)	84
Toby Robinson (10)	86

Nadia Timuri (10)	87
Melissa Mills (9)	88
Hamish Tulleth (9)	89
Rae Wells (10)	90
Lottie Newton (7)	91
Yousef Mohammedi (7)	92
Ruby-May Howard (8)	93
Livia Barros (7)	94
Isla-Mae Guy (8)	95
Megha Mahesh (8)	96
Thomas Bartlett (9)	97
Dixie Weake (8)	98
Rex Inns (8)	99
Adam Bessaih (7)	100
Stanley Goodwin (8)	101
Jessica Hardy (8)	102
Stella Davey (9)	103
Ellie Hlinican (8)	104

St Mary's CE Primary School, Barnsley

Mia Watkin (8)	105
Sophia Cassell (9)	106
Georgia Rose Peace (8)	108
Teddy Cassell (8)	110
Gracie Gibbons (9)	111
Elva Clegg (9)	112
Sherry Liang (9)	113
Georgia Skidmore (9)	114
Emily Hodgkinson (9)	115
India Ibbeson (8)	116
Tobias Sekanina (9)	117
Amarachi Eze (8)	118
Zach Morgan (8)	119
Vanesa Jokimciute (9)	120
Jack Thornton (9)	121
Theo Gaskell-Booth (9)	122
Borys Patyk (9)	123
Rose Karimi (9)	124
Lailah Braithwaite (9)	125
Johana Jintu (8)	126

St Thomas CE (VC) Primary School, Bradley

Sienna-Marie Roberts (10)	127
Dae'naja Bedeau (10)	128
Joshua Norman-Mcleoud (10)	129
Josh Stead (10)	130

Tavernspite Community Primary School, Whitland

Lowri Thomas (11)	131
Mischa Orford (11)	132
Spencer Reynolds (11)	135
Pippa Thomas (11)	136
Jack Leyfield (11)	138
Cedi Michael (11)	139
Harri H	140
Matty May (10)	141
Elsie Fowler (11)	142

Two Gates Community Primary School, Two Gates

Erin Simkins (9)	143
Georgie-May Haynes (10)	144
Olivia May Kidd (9)	145
Rayyan Chaudhry (10)	146

Whitchurch Primary School & Nursery, Stanmore

Siya Samani (8)	147
Trisha Bhatnagar (11)	148
Shrien Varsani (10)	150
Sefora Matis Bumb (9)	152
Reeva Rabadiya (9)	153
Hriday Patel (9)	154
Anahi Lily Gandhi-Mehta (9)	155
Prince Patel (10)	156

White Notley CE (VC) Primary School, White Notley

Jessica Naylor (8)	157
Isabella Sapienza (8)	158
Amaia Franklin (8)	159
Maya Kassan-Lawrence (9)	160

THE CREATIVE WRITING

Amazing Tigers

Terrific tigers trample through the mystical woods
Interesting tigers roll through the soggy mud.
Wrecking leaves with their really sharp claws
Gargantuan tigers stride through the misty jungles
Every type of tiger, I love!

Tahlia (8)

Teacher Creature

Pacing down the corridor
My heart thumping fast
Feeling like a foreigner
I can't find my class

What should I do?
Things are out of the blue
I find my room
I rush, my homework is due!

The class is empty
Something is not right
My legs turn to jelly
I clench my fists tight

Where is my teacher?
The classroom is deserted
What is this creature?
My attention is diverted

Is that my classmate?
Moving past my eye
A figure so straight
Creepy not wise!

Standing still when I look
Moving at me when I don't
I feel something on my foot
A face bony and toned

A horrendous face!
Snap, snap, I hear her clap
My heart speeds up a pace
Her fingers snap!

As tall as a tree
Nails long and sharp
That scrape and screech
She's scary and smart

Tick, tick, tock the clock goes
Touching her glasses
A devilish smile grows
She turns to ashes

My sister shouts
Get up now!
I see her pout
I still smell ashes...
Wow...

Ayesha Qadri (9)
Batley Parish CE Primary Academy, Batley

End Of The Forest

All around me, lots of green
There's nobody else, to be seen
The wind blows, I feel the breeze
Towering over me, the tall, tall trees
In the distance, the clouds growl
Right below me, something smells foul
I tread on further, into the gloomy air
Moving the branches, out of my hair
Spiky leaves, poke through my skin
I feel no pain, but the bleeding begin
The whistling wind, calls my name
I go in deeper, to the screams of rain
My body shivers, goosebumps appear
Rolling down my cheek, I feel a tear
Where am I? My heart beats fast
Is this the end? Is this the last?
There's no going back
Everything is black.

Najeebah Mayat (9)
Batley Parish CE Primary Academy, Batley

My Running Race

I'm on the starting line
I'm not feeling fine
I feel sick
I have to be quick
The blue whistle blows
And off I go
Everybody is so fast
I don't want to come last
So I speed up my pace
My heart starts to race
I can do this, I can win
I just need to believe in myself
I'm nervous and I'm scared
I'm glad that I prepared
I'm close to the finish line
I need a good time
I have to sprint and speed up my pace
I have overtaken the girl
And I'm in first place,
Everyone is cheering so loud,
And my mum is very proud.

Isabella Walker (9)
Batley Parish CE Primary Academy, Batley

The Dark Night

In the shadows deep, where nightmares dwell, a realm of worries where the darkness swells. In the slumber, horror will play and haunting dreams that lead astray. A chilling wind, an eerie moan, tears running down my face. I wander all alone with every step, my heart dreads and I wonder when I can go back to bed.
In the abyss, the winds beckon my name and their eyes glow with an icy stare. A nightmare that makes me shiver, every moment that goes by, the sky seems dimmer. My heart pounds faster as I wonder, *will I ever wake up from this horror?*

Sanaa Sidat (9)
Batley Parish CE Primary Academy, Batley

Journey On The Whale

I went to the seaside with my family
To enjoy the cool waves openly
My feet inside the water
Felt ticklish under
Something touched on my feet like a cat's tail
I realised I was pushed up by the whales
With one foot on the whale's body
And another on the other whale's body
Whales dived into the water, throwing me into stream
Splashes of water woke me up from my dream
Ah! I was on the carpet; fallen from bed
The beautiful journey was not real, a dream instead.

Asad Kamran (8)
Batley Parish CE Primary Academy, Batley

Once Upon A Dream

Once upon a dream, I had a nightmare
As frightening as can be
Without a sound, a wizard flew through my room with a broom
A wizard flying in my room?
I woke up and I was lost
I heard a car go vroom
I saw a dragon which said hello
I ran to the door nice and slow
Lost and confused, in a nightmare
There I was stuck with my pet duck
As I was trying to escape I saw something in the distance
It was a book.

Jamielee Glover (9)
Batley Parish CE Primary Academy, Batley

Enchanted Forest

In a forest full of life,
There are mushrooms that are white,
Magical fairies also thrive,
Alongside animals far and wide,
Rivers and streams flow tranquilly,
Why do I feel so still and calm?
A slight wind blows my arm,
There are plants all around,
It's so peaceful and there's not a sound.

Holly Cooke (9)
Batley Parish CE Primary Academy, Batley

Little Kangaroo

I am a little kangaroo, jumping up and down.
I like to eat grass, leaves, ferns, flowers and fruit.
We chew our food twice before it passes through our small stomachs.
I am a little kangaroo, jumping up and down.

Muhammed Bin Anas (9)
Batley Parish CE Primary Academy, Batley

The Fantastic Dreambox

I wake up in my room to find,
A peculiar box sits on my windowsill,
Where has it come from? Why is it here?
I just don't know, but is this a trick?
So I take a risky step forward, then a risky step back,
In the blinding moonlight, the box seems to open,
A fairy comes and flies beside,
And asks me, "What do you see?"
I am then lost in my dreams,
I see... dragons gliding through the treetops,
Fireflies light the midnight sky
Unicorns, spiders and wizards everywhere!
And magical flowers all in a row,
The Dreambox is swirling with myths and magic,
Colours of all fill my head,
But nightmares are invading, oh no!
Am I still in bed?
But there is an explosion of mystics,
My eyes flicker like mad,
And I am soon awake in the morning,
That was an adventure, I'll find Mum and Dad!

Amber Dyer (8)
Cuddington And Dinton CE School, Dinton

Candy Land

As I drift off into my dream
Nothing is quite as real as it seems
Dogs begin to flutter
Around the arena with fur as smooth as butter
The horses take flight
The dogs are way out of sight
As I sit with my friend
And they hope there'll be no end
Candyfloss floating
We're in for a showing
We're going and going
To get much closer
They'll never know what's coming
It is going to be funny
Everyone was laughing
They knew that the day was coming to an end
But they still had one thing coming
Well, one big thing happening
They hopped in the carriage
And flew over lollipops, gumdrops, candyfloss
The surprise was a big party
They partied all night

But now it was morning
And a fresh start to a new day
Forget about yesterday
Think about the present, not the past

Winnie Bernstein (8)
Cuddington And Dinton CE School, Dinton

Once Upon A Dream

Once upon a dream,
I sat nearby a stream,
And all of a sudden,
I heard a slight fluttering of fairies twinkling all around me.
A creature came up to me,
Unknowingly unicorns were twinkling,
Across the fascinating view blocking up,
Secrets throughout my mind,
Scrambling into distant secrets.
Warming my heart artistically,
Looking at my art,
Across the pages above my heart.

My thoughts are random in my dreams,
Picking up secrets, travelling overseas.
Round in circles, dropping off words in a peaceful calm place,
A place that's amazing, fantastic, brilliant, wonderful.

My eyes start to flutter as the sun gets close by,
And I awake from my dreaming with a wonderful smile.

Amara Sewell (8)
Cuddington And Dinton CE School, Dinton

Imagination

I n your imagination, you can do whatever you want
M agic flows through your mind
A nything is possible, this isn't the end of the world
G et ready for your mind to blow
I magine your way through the good and the bad
N othing can stop you from achieving your dreams
A nyone, anything, can be there with you
T hink of the future
I gnite your dreams
O nly you can control your imagination
N ow go, run free with your dreams!

Rosie Allen (7)
Cuddington And Dinton CE School, Dinton

When I Was A Bird

One day, as I was going to bed,
I fell over and banged my head.
I tried to get up, but something was wrong,
My arms were all feathery, and my mouth chirped a song!
I ran to my mum, and I wanted to cry,
But when I opened my arms, I started to fly!
My mum said, "What's going on? Get into bed!"
So I flew over her and pooed on her head.
She started to shout and started to scream,
And then I woke up and it was all a dream.

Aria Delnevo (7)
Cuddington And Dinton CE School, Dinton

Dream Birds

D ramatic birds swooping through the air
R omantic parrots flying calmly
E merald parakeets sitting on branches
A iming to be free
M editating eagles resting on their nests.

B eautiful colours high in the sky
I nteresting to see
R apidly bursting through the sky
D amp and cold, they're wide awake
S ilently flying through the air.

Eva Reng (7)
Cuddington And Dinton CE School, Dinton

Bunnies

B ouncing bunnies go hop, hop, hop
U nderground, they live snuggled up together
N aughty little things, eating our vegetables
N ice things for pets, except the vegetable problem
I have to say they're amazingly cute
E very animal loves them, except the predator fox
S cary things for carrots, (not saying they're real!).

Amelie Smith (8)
Cuddington And Dinton CE School, Dinton

If I Had A Dog

If I had my own pet dog,
I'd cuddle her every day,
I'd stroke her, tickle her, rub her tum
And every day we'd play.

I'd throw a ball for her to catch,
I'd take her for a walk,
I'd teach her lots of clever tricks
And even teach her how to talk.

I'd feed her a treat,
So she'd jump off her feet.

So... please, please, please, please can I have a dog?

Clara Wilby (8)
Cuddington And Dinton CE School, Dinton

Mermaid

M agical and marvellous was the day I was a mermaid.
E vidently, they were proven not to be real, but they were wrong.
R adiant was the sun that day.
M um said I could play in a wave.
A mazing I had a tail and flippers.
I nteresting was the world under the sea.
D iving back up to the surface, my tail had gone.

Vivienne Douglass (8)
Cuddington And Dinton CE School, Dinton

Fairy Bunnies

Fairy bunnies flutter around,
But they don't want to be seen or found.
If you dare... they will pull out your hair!
They eat carrots galore,
And when they go to sleep, they do a big snore!
Now if one looks at you in the eye,
They will declare a fight!
£5 bill but they still won't pay.
Because they think that they will save the day!

Thea Andrew (8)
Cuddington And Dinton CE School, Dinton

Supercars

S uper Lamborghini speeding around the track
U p and down the course I go
P owerful and flash!
E veryone is jealous of my supercar
R acing round the F1 track
C ars can't catch me now
A re you jealous of my car? It's
R eally, really cool
S uper Lamborghini driving me to school.

Henry Rush (8)
Cuddington And Dinton CE School, Dinton

The Battle

A monster in a cave
Dark and cold
Here comes a dragon
Dangerous and ferocious

The fight begins
The dragon breathes fire
The monster is not defeated
But the dragon is

A spirit blesses the dragon
And it comes back to life.

Christopher (7)
Cuddington And Dinton CE School, Dinton

Magic

M ysterious and mythical moonlight power,
A ncient arts awaken the dark,
G lorious glittering orbs reveal the hour,
I n deep forests, blood-red foxes bark,
C ome to the magical enchanted tower.

Josh Davis (8)
Cuddington And Dinton CE School, Dinton

The Nature Boy

The nature boy is a boy who had a wonderful dream
It started with a beautiful gleam
It led him to a wonderful place
Then it started to speed up so he gave chase
It took him to a deep dark hole
In there was a magnificent bear eating a vole
At that moment he heard a voice in his head:
"People have stopped to care
It's filling me with despair"
With that, he went outside
He said, "Where did your family go?"
"They died," the bear replied
He went deeper into the wild
He felt cold, even though the air was quite mild
In the distance, he saw tractors ripping up trees
Beyond that were the seas
At that moment, he realised it wasn't his time
So he went up a tree, and even further away, there was a mine!

Daniel Ball (9)
Fossebrook Primary School, Leicester

My Day At The Vets

My day at the vets was wonderful!
Cats meowing in my ear all day,
Nibbling on my fingers,
Turns out they just wanted to play!
They just wanted to play!

I gave them treats,
And I gave them cuddles,
Uh oh!
They've got all muddled!
They've got all muddled!

Oh no! What happened?
I tried calling their names,
But that didn't work,
They all looked the same!
They all looked the same!

That one's Puzzle and that one Dusty!
That's Mittens and this is Mila!
That one's Lily and that one's Minnie!
That's Misty and this is Lila!
This is Lila!

Yay!
I did it, I cracked the case!
They were so happy,
They started licking my face!
Licking my face!

Suddenly something happened!
It was Mittens!
Something popped out,
She had 8 kittens!
She had 8 kittens!

Anarra Lakhani (9)
Fossebrook Primary School, Leicester

The Scary Nightmare

Once upon a time, a man was walking through the woods. He was a bit scared, but thought, *toughen up, Chuck!* He kept walking and he met a clown. He ran for his life, he was terrified. He looked behind him and the clown had vanished. He calmed down, but then the clown popped up again out of nowhere! The clown caught him.

The clown put him in a cell. There were clowns surrounding him with metal bats. Then, the clowns were gone, they teleported. So he had a chance to escape. He managed to escape but the thing was, he didn't know the way out.

He searched for two days, and eventually, he found the way out. He escaped and then he ran through the woods like Usain Bolt. Finally, he got home. He told himself that he would never go through those woods again. Never.

Freddie Dulon (8)
Fossebrook Primary School, Leicester

Clowny Night

C harming sleeps, everybody loves it
L ong before the clown with its big, white robe wakes up
O h wow, oh no, the clown with the creepy smile is coming
W ith its creepy smile, it scares me
N ow it is in the room, the clown with its bloody hands slowly picks me up
Y eet! The clown with its bloodshot eyes throws me to the ground

N ow the clown with its creepy laugh wakes my parents
I t's the clown with the weird, funky boots, Mum
G reat, says the clown with its creepy stare flying away
H i, said the clown with its long stare
T onight I was prepared, I got a bat. It can't creep me out now.

Lucas-James Gaskin Yurt (9)
Fossebrook Primary School, Leicester

Bad Things

The people who are bad
Are the people who make you sad
The people who lie
Are the people who make you cry
You cry
You cry
The people who make you cry

The things that you get
These are the people who make you upset
And when you get upset they will make you more depressed
Depressed
Depressed
They are the people who make you depressed

But when they get sad, don't be bad
Lift them up and just give them a hug
A hug
A hug
Just give them a hug
Then there's a thud
And they turn out to be good
Then you become friends

And it might turn out
Or it might stay, but if it ends
Just, live your way.

Lewis Woodward (9)
Fossebrook Primary School, Leicester

The Tiger

There was a knock at my door and it was a small, cute tiger and I had to let it in. But when I searched for what type of tiger it was, I couldn't believe it because it was the most expensive tiger in the world and I took a picture and put it on TikTok. I got £500,000 from it, plus another £100,000 and I bought a mansion that cost me £100,000. I bought three bodyguards and some food for my little, cute tiger and I went to my friend's house. I couldn't believe that he had more money than me! So I said, "Give me half and I will give you my Lamborghini." He didn't know that I had a Bugatti, so he said yes and I became the most popular person on the internet.

Olly Marsden (9)
Fossebrook Primary School, Leicester

There's A Monkey At The Door

There was a knock at my door, oh, who could it be?
I opened the door and all I could see
Was a big monkey
The monkey was buff
And he was tough
He shouted, "Boom!"
So I headed to my living room
He smashed the door
With a bash and a crash
Glass shards were flying everywhere
The monkey stared at me with a deathly stare
I didn't know what to do
The monkey said, "I need you to get me a banana
For my treat, or I will throw you on the street
You know I will, my name's Biu
I used to live in a zoo
I'm not joking, it's true
I normally lie
When I eat pie."

Riley Gledhill (9)
Fossebrook Primary School, Leicester

The Fox And Pussycat

There was a fox and a pussycat. They went on a brown boat. The fox looked at the stars. "Oh, dear pussycat, you're the best. Oh, pussycat, I love you. Oh, we should get married!"
A year later and they were still on the boat. They wanted to get married. They both saw a pig. It had a ring on its nose.
"The nose."
"The nose."
"The nose."
"Do you have a ring on your nose? Are you selling it? Because I would like to take it!"
Then they got married and lived, "Happily, happily, happily."

Sienna Farmer (8)
Fossebrook Primary School, Leicester

Fears

F or once, I don't recognise anything I see,
E verything is different, as different as can be,
A t last, I see something crawling through the shadows,
R aging and shouting, creeping through the meadows,
S omething touches me, it's a creepy, scary clown.

F eeling scared, I walk back,
E nvy on the clown's face, he wants me as a snack,
A ll I know begins to disappear,
R eeking smells come through,
S o for once, I'm filled with fear...

Julia Kilinska (8)
Fossebrook Primary School, Leicester

The Dead Dog

Sebastian stepped out in a mood,
The dead dog was shining in the moon,
It had been glued to a flower that bloomed,
I called the police and said, "The dog is clearly dead,"
They rushed to the hospital and said, "The dog is dead,"
The hospital said, "The dog is actually dead,"
The boy said, "Put him in a bed,"
The hospital said, "No, he is dead,"
Then the police shouted, "I will bury him with the dead."

Emerson Vickers-Hunt (9)
Fossebrook Primary School, Leicester

The Singer's Vocalist

I want to be a singer, but which type should I be?
Rock 'n' roll, hip-hop, I don't know what to choose
Oh dear me!
I don't know what I shall be

Oh no, it's my first concert
When should I start and why would I be
I started and everyone would flee

That was a little long
I mean it's been four years
I've made millions of songs
So I've made some attempts
Boom! And...
I was meant to be!

Marysia Buk (9)
Fossebrook Primary School, Leicester

The Four Girls And The Four Elements

There were four girls who had powers:
Earth,
Fire,
Water,
Air.

In the blink of an eye:
Fire came,
Earth came,
Water came,
Air came.

Out of the blue,
There was an intruder.
Fire hit him,
Earth put a rock wall around him,
Water made a tsunami,
Air made a tornado.

The intruder came again,
And their evil brothers came too,
Fire appeared,
And ended their lives.

Jake Goodwin (8)
Fossebrook Primary School, Leicester

The Robotic Lizard

Once upon a time, there was a boy called Spencer. Spencer was a great boy. He had much joy.
One day, he came up with an idea. A nice idea. A couple of years later, he tried to build. He tried and tried. He really tried. He failed. After a couple of encouragements, he became creative and creative was what he was.
He thought about it. He wanted to save the country, so he added weapons. Blades, guns, an atomic beam, rockets and a beam that came out of the chest.

Spencer Williams (9)
Fossebrook Primary School, Leicester

The Fear Of A Lifetime

Terror rings throughout the halls,
I find myself standing straight and tall
My body braces to face this sight,
It's a demon, shaded by twilight,
The blood-red eyes had a demonic look,
I was too scared, this was the last hook,
It stepped towards me, silver fangs bared,
It met my eyes with its deathly stare,
I walked, I ran, and then I quickly fled...
Then suddenly, I found myself safe in bed.

Yashasvi Dadhich (9)
Fossebrook Primary School, Leicester

Superpower To The City

Superpowers struck a rampage on the city
Maybe the lightning was a bit early
Laser beams struck the high pointy cliffs
Oops the fires are burning the forest
At least water was able to save it
Oh no, levitation struck the city, we were all floating
Luckily, gravity was able to save it
Brightness struck the city, maybe a bit... too bright
At last, darkness struck and we were back to normal.

Ifeoluwa Alabi (9)
Fossebrook Primary School, Leicester

My Nightmare About MH370

Planes go high, planes go low
But I boarded one that became aviation's foe
MH370 is high in the sky
But then plunges down like a dead fly
Lights are out, people cry
As MH370 falls out of the sky
"No fuel, no fuel!" the pilot shouts
As the triple seven shoots out of its route
I burst into the cockpit but it is too late
The terrain alarm goes off, time to accept my fate.

Aleksander Ryzner (9)
Fossebrook Primary School, Leicester

The Spaceship

The spaceship came whizzing by,
And took them one by one.
Goodbye; lots of people disappeared.
It was caught by the news reporter,
And it was all over the news,
And the police went to investigate,
Where they got taken,
Because it showed them taking them.
They could shape-shift,
So they might get away.
You might have gotten away,
But you won't be so lucky next time.

Jonah Goodwin (8)
Fossebrook Primary School, Leicester

Going To North Korea

Once upon a dream,
I went to North Korea,
With my family and aunty,
I went through a portal,
There was no one except my family,
The city was like a wallpaper,
It was like a boring paper,
We were a bit looney,
It was gloomy,
We were not really crazy,
The people were lazy,
The clouds weren't in the sky,
The people weren't loud,
But we were loud.

Enrico Chauhan-Gerace (8)
Fossebrook Primary School, Leicester

The School Trip

Once upon a time,
There was a rhyme,
A school bus committed a crime.
Lucas was a curse,
That the teachers hurt.
The bus went through a portal,
But the struggling students were hurt.
"Don't worry," said Lolly,
You will be alright.

"Where are we?"
"There is another portal over there," said the bear.
"Let's go!"

Lucas Odedra (9)
Fossebrook Primary School, Leicester

The Plastic Apocalypse

Once upon a dream,
The world was a team,
We all need to help,
Before the planet melts,
Use a bin,
Recycle a tin,
Don't waste paper,
Use it later,
Don't litter plastic,
So our world will be fantastic,
So can you see?
There is no planet B,
All these microscopic bits,
It's the plastic apocalypse...

Ava Stokes (9)
Fossebrook Primary School, Leicester

Sixty-Six Million Years Back To The Dinosaurs

I made a time machine.
And went back to sixty-six million years to the age of the dinosaurs.
I arrived in the Cretaceous period.
I saw a T-rex attacking an allosaurus,
And the allosaurus tried to attack me back.
And another T-rex saved me.

Johnpaul Shaju (9)
Fossebrook Primary School, Leicester

Writer

There was a little girl named Lizzy and her twin named Lily. Lizzy was the smarter one and Lily loved to write ever since she was little. She was three when she could write, but one day, she ran away because her sister got more attention than Lily.

Thea Rodgers (9)
Fossebrook Primary School, Leicester

Famous

    F or you are dreams
    A nice dream, a bad dream
    M esmerising, magical dreams
    O f course the dreams are different
Yo **U** can make it different, have the
    S ame dream if you want.

Oseana James-O'Callaghan (9)
Fossebrook Primary School, Leicester

Greedy Jenny

Greedy Jenny ate some fish and some porridge in a dish,
She ate some apples and some bananas, too many.

Greedy Jenny saw some muffins in the fridge and could not stop craving them,
Greedy Jenny ate some muffins and yoghurt in a fridge.

Greedy Jenny saw Peter eating doughnuts and asked for the doughnuts too,
She ate some grapes and some biscuits too.

Now Greedy Jenny could not walk, her stomach was aching,
Greedy Jenny started vomiting,
Suddenly, she was crying,
Oh, poor Greedy Jenny!
She was taken to hospital.

Nozinhle Nyoni (9)
Holy Cross Catholic Primary School, Liverpool

Flowers And Stars

Watch them grow, it might take a while
Just look at the sun shine bright
Just when it is night
The moon puts light on the shining stars
The owls howl as we hear flies zoom
As the other side of the moon appears
And the sun slowly appears
As the flowers are back in sight
Watch the purple blossoms bloom
And the sunflowers rise
And the daisies open up
When I see flowers
I feel like there is
An energetic butterfly in my brain
I love flowers
I have some daisies in my garden
When I feel sad
I remember
When the daisies were seeds
And now they are huge
I water them every day
(Weekends).

My message to the world:
"Don't think about what anyone thinks, you be you."
Sometimes, I think, *what if no one likes flowers?*
But even if no one likes flowers, well, I like flowers and that is all that matters.

Sasha Mswelanto (8)
Holy Cross Catholic Primary School, Liverpool

Dreams

D ancing together all day long, and it is good with a song
R acing every day to the park, we do it until it is dark
E very night we dream, until it seems that it is day
A mazing wizards, amazing lizards
M onkeys seem cool, dripped in jewels
S eems to be that every night we have a dream, and sometimes in it we can be keen. All of these can be in dreams, and if you tell it, it can be seen.

Willow-Rose Fearns (9)
Holy Cross Catholic Primary School, Liverpool

A World Of...

A world of dragons, fairies and unicorns; bright on the outside, but when you say goodnight, it's a real fright. Unicorns and fairies turn into goblins and zombies, dragons hide for their lives. You can hear screeches and squeaks of the imperfect creatures while they kill the dragons (they did nothing wrong). The next morning, the dead dragons are gone. Maybe to another world? No one knows. The unicorns and fairies act like nothing happened while the dragons are distraught and relieved that they survived. Still, no dragon has the heart to fight, even the ones with fierce and strong hearts won't.

Ellie Moore (11)
Le Cateau Community Primary School, Catterick Garrison

Flowers Of All

Bluebells and daisies wave on rolling fields,
You feel at ease, but there's one still.
Motionless and dark, its colours fade,
The clouds emerge as the sun turns into shade.
The lone flower weeps, back to being sad,
Flowers dip down as the lonely flower cries.
All colour and happiness come to die.
A beam of light comes into view, and red petals of rubies flicker with glee.
They come together,
Light be dark,
They create life and death for the rest.
Life and death live with us,
So respect the rows of roses and corpses.

Lily Robinson (11)
Le Cateau Community Primary School, Catterick Garrison

Dream

I know I am in a dream,

I know I am in a dream,
When I am running down a chocolate stream.

Kids running to the ends of rainbows,
And little girls wearing big red bows.

It is raining cats and dogs,
And the land is filled with big blue frogs.

Big yellow butterflies,
As the sun is about to rise.

Pink skies about to turn green,
As you do the Michael Jackson lean.

Cotton candy clouds,
Surrounded by crowds.

Hope Eveson (11)
Le Cateau Community Primary School, Catterick Garrison

Once Upon A Dream

Once upon a dream
I went to school
But today something was different
It wasn't very cool!

I walked into the classroom
And saw my teacher there
As well as lots of animals
Including a polar bear!

Isla was a llama
Oscar was a monkey
Olivia was a kangaroo
She was very jumpy

Elizabeth was a polar bear
Lottie was a cat
Joey had a really long tail
Because he was a rat!

Sienna was a bird
Oakley was a dog
Sophie was a red and blue
Poisonous dart frog!

Lewis was a giraffe
Carter was a mouse
Ruby was a snail
She carried her own house!

Leighton was a wolf
Ellis was a pig
Lexi was a mole
Who always wanted to dig!

Musaad was a lion
Rihanna was a moose
Austin was a big, white,
Feathery, brown-eyed goose

I looked in the mirror
And couldn't believe my eyes
What I saw looking back at me
Was a big surprise!

My ears were long and fluffy
My tail was the shape of a ball
My fur was grey and white
I was the best animal of all

I was a *rabbit!*

Ella Hands (9)
Provost Williams CofE Primary School, Coventry

Safe And Sound, Or Is It?

I was in my room drifting slowly off to sleep.
My dream was so scary, I wished I could leap.
Out of bed, out of my room,
Onto the moon.

I closed my eyes and dozed.
I found myself in a ground of thunder-struck trees.
I wished I had good luck with the weather.
I squeezed my teddy as soft as a feather.
It was roaring with thunder, pouring with rain.
The silk spiderwebs spelt out my name.

I found a monster made of slime,
"Oh no! I've just realised the time."
It was midnight.
That means there will be no light.

I wanted my family.
Rather than be in this scary gallery.
I tossed and turned in my bed.
I didn't want to end this adventure dead.

Oh no, the monster caught me.
I must have been too slow.
Roar. Roar. Roar.
Suddenly, I woke.
The roaring was my mother and brother.
Playing dinosaurs.
I looked at the date.
It was Monday, I was going to be late.
For school.

Sienna Gardner (9)
Provost Williams CofE Primary School, Coventry

Backrooms

B lack in the backrooms sooty as dark paint everything was raven.
A nd all was the same. I got all sucked in just like dry paint.
C an't get out, I'm all in a state. Could I get out?
K now I couldn't even though I tried, and all I ate was a little tiny tyre. I was
R ich, so I called my bodyguard, but he was dealing with Mitch so he couldn't.
O ur friend was lost, I was worried, just like Cox, then I found my friend.
O ur mother was lost, somewhere in here, even though his other friend was here.
M y mother she is, she is... don't know where she is, I was looking around, then
S he was there, she was, worried, sorry we are in a rush let's go. Mother! No!

Joey Mcgovern (9)
Provost Williams CofE Primary School, Coventry

Elizabeth's Dream

Once upon a dream, I was on a tropical island,
The sun was beaming like a happy child,
The sky was blue and the sea was clear,
The light would guide through on a warm sunny day,
Then suddenly fairies came and swam in the sea,
The ice cream van came and the fairies and I got ice cream,
After the ice cream, we danced on the beach,
We were dancing as magnificently as dancers,
Then the fairy queen turned me into a fairy,
Then I explored the fairy palace,
In the palace there was gold and statues, some were old, some were new,
I had tea and cake, and then I turned back into a human.

Elizabeth Tasker (9)
Provost Williams CofE Primary School, Coventry

The Great Left Foot Power Shot

I'm in the match,
Trying to attack,
The great trophy of gold,
To reward me for being bold.

They've got a free-kick,
It's time for a trick,
I'm in the great, strong wall,
Trying my hardest to block the ball.

I'm dribbling quite fast,
Past the defender who's last,
I shoot my hardest for a power shot,
Though it is my hat-trick shot.

I'm celebrating with my family,
Cheering me under the canopy,
I lift up the great trophy of gold,
High up into the night of cold.

This is the best time of my life,
Underneath the moon of light,
I'm in the match,
With the trophy attached.

Oakley Cox (9)
Provost Williams CofE Primary School, Coventry

The Murderer

Once I went to the shop
To buy a can of pop
Me and my best friend
Went around the bend
Into an alley
Where we saw a man with a hat by Sally
Blood splattered on his face
Next thing I saw was my friend running with pace
I turned around
To hear no sound
Everything went black
I was in a sack
He took me to a house
Where I could see a mouse
His deathly sneer
Filled me with fear
I had died
Then the man was trying to hide.
If only I'd stayed away
I would have lived to see another day.

Sophie Dudley (9)
Provost Williams CofE Primary School, Coventry

The World's Scariest Adventure

I went to a haunted house,
But little did I know...
It was haunted,
I went inside the house,
But the door slammed shut right behind me,
Suddenly, the lights started to flicker,
The curtains closed,
The windows closed,
The drains got blocked,
The taps turned on,
All the electricity went out,
Even the fireplace turned off,
I tried to run out of the house,
But the door was locked,
I tried the back door and the windows,
But they were locked too...

Musaad Saiyed (9)
Provost Williams CofE Primary School, Coventry

The Dream Team

F irst onto the field sprinted I,
O ver my head, I threw the ball high,
O llie Watkins came running quickly onto the grass,
T hen McGinn came to take our penalty,
B ailey came racing onto the field to score,
A mazingly, the ball came to me,
L egs strong, I rock the show, then I score,
L ots of shouting and cheering,
E veryone was not doubting,
R aising the golden Champions League trophy. We won!

Oscar Maunder (9)
Provost Williams CofE Primary School, Coventry

The Great Right Foot

A ll of the players wait
T aking the penalty, he scores
H ere comes Lewis, the star boy
L egs big and strong; focus, free-kick, scores!
E veryone goes crazy
T hey celebrate 100 goals
E veryone cheers his name: Lewis the legend.

Lewis Young (8)
Provost Williams CofE Primary School, Coventry

Different Is Good

Once upon a dream,
I dreamt of a girl,
Who got bullied by some people,
She got bullied because she was different,
But different is good and bullying isn't,

Once upon a dream,
I dreamt of a girl,
Who didn't have any friends,
She didn't have friends because she looked different,
Different is good, but being unkind isn't,

Once upon a dream,
I dreamt of a girl,
Who sat at a table all alone,
She sometimes got mocked because she was different,
Different is good, but treating other people like this isn't,

Once upon a dream,
I dreamt of a girl who was ignored,
She was ignored because her skin colour was different,
Different is good, but discriminating against others isn't.

Rachel Moulder (11)
St Eanswythe's CE Primary School, Folkestone

The Giant In My Dream

In my dreams every night,
I am sometimes woken to fight.
Sometimes there are horses and fish,
Or other times a genie grants my wish.
Last night something came to me,
There was a giant planting a tree.
He began to walk away,
But I decided to stay.
I began to walk to the plant,
Then there was a noise like a chant.
The chant went like this,
In a cloud of mist.
Meet me after one day,
But there may be a price to pay.
Dreams are the canvas where our minds create,
A world of wonder where anything is fate.
So close your eyes and let your mind be free,
And see what your dreams can be.

Pixie Faulkner (11)
St Eanswythe's CE Primary School, Folkestone

Magical Creatures

When I go to bed at night,
My body gets an awful fright.
Magical creatures blind my eyes
And they make my mind feel mesmerised.
The magical creatures prance in the air,
As they twirl and whirl with such flair.
Their eyes glisten like ice on fire,
As my dreams wander higher and higher.
My dreams can take me to outer space,
Where the creatures put on a magical show which lights up my face.
They laugh and giggle all through the night,
And sometimes make me feel alright.
Maybe you could have my dream,
And see the moonlight gleam.

Autumn McCairn (11)
St Eanswythe's CE Primary School, Folkestone

Dreams Of Nothing

Dreams turn as black as a cold heart
Power runs away in a broken cart
Nothing is left but bone and skin
Dignity walks away with a grin
Run, run, the nightmare's coming.

Dreams shatter beyond repair
Evil villains plan and prepare
Nothing but terror and a good scare
Bar one sitting high in thine own chair
Run, run, the nightmare's coming.

Keira Murphy (11)
St Eanswythe's CE Primary School, Folkestone

It Was Just A Dream

I closed my drifting eyes
Late at night
All tucked up and cosy
Only my dreams in sight.

Floating high in the sky
Above the clouds
Lay a football field
I could hear the crowds.

I couldn't believe my eyes
Players flying high in the air and
The opposing team
Fire-breathing dragons everywhere.

The deafening whistle
Piercing all our ears
And the football players
Had to face their fears.

The charging ball swivelled
Across the field
It looked like
The players were given a shield.

I opened my eyes
And I looked around
But I couldn't find out
Who had won the round.

Leo Hegarty (10)
St Francis Primary School, Lurgan

Candy Land

If you close your eyes and go to sleep
There's a special place you will want to creep
A place of wonder and magic too
Candy Land is waiting for you!

A little Freddo Frog jumps out of a hot chocolate pond
While jelly babies dance and fly with their wands
Marshmallow clouds float high in the sky
With a giant sourball sun when it is nice and dry.

There are candy cane trees in the Matchmaker grass
And when it rains, it's gumdrops and everyone laughs
A gingerbread house, so yummy and sweet
Oh, come to Candy Land and you'll be in for a treat!

Luca Goddard (10)
St Francis Primary School, Lurgan

My Dreams And Wishes

Every time I go to bed at night,
I just might dream of a light,
A light so bright from far beyond,
Like stars reflecting in a pond.

My dreams take me far and wide,
To a sunny beach with a tide,
From Spain and Egypt, maybe Thailand too!
As they say, our dreams do come true,
Let them be in our hands,
Some day I'll be in the golden sand.

Wherever we are, we always dream,
Sometimes they make you scream,
Other times they make you cry so much,
You need ice cream.

But so long, it's still a dream.

Emma Cullen (10)
St Francis Primary School, Lurgan

Where Am I?

I am in a dream,
A mythical forest,
Creatures surround me,
Not having a single clue where I am,
Animals talk and laugh,
Two fat boys are arguing,
There is so much more,
But one with a hat I caught running away,
He invites me to the table,
With more and more mysterious creatures,
Cards come after us,
I somehow shrink into the 9/10 hat,
But still,
I don't know where I am...

Grace McAnarney (10)
St Francis Primary School, Lurgan

Once Upon A Dream

Once upon a dream, the stars shone bright.
Once upon a dream, the moon was my light.
Once upon a dream, I lay in my bed
With my teddy by my side and my pillow at my head.
Once upon a dream, the owl was awake
As the fish swam quietly through the lake
Right until daybreak.

Lily Jane Monaghan (10)
St Francis Primary School, Lurgan

A Nightmare

Fly high
Like a butterfly
Cry like a cat with no eyes
Sometimes you realise
That your hellos turn
Into byes
Forever and ever
Will I dream with no screams?
Like a nightmare
With no lights?

Sofia Murray (10)
St Francis Primary School, Lurgan

Sweet Dreams

I close my eyes and try to sleep,
I aim to drift off and count twenty sheep.
As soon as I feel I have tried everything,
I fall into dreams with a faint-sounding *ping*.
My eyes are now open and there's sugar all around,
There's even fluffy candyfloss standing in for the ground.
The trees seem to be made of smooth silk chocolate,
And ice cream cones, fully ready to collect.
There are lakes of caramel and sandpits of sherbet,
And there's even a statue of my pet hamster, Herbet.
But over in the valley, I see quite a sight,
And when I think back now, it shines so bright.
A house and garden made entirely of candy,
My stomach says that might just come in handy.
Oh no! My alarm! It's 7:30am!
Now I have to get out of bed again.

Chloe Ross (10)
St Mark's Primary School, Hanwell

Bloody Nightmares

Your nightmare comes before you go to sleep. The nightmare starts... *now!* There's blood in my eyes, cracking each bone with my best friend. We find each other, but there's still more ahead. Bloody Mary comes out from the dark, trying to kill us. *"Please! Help!"* I pinch myself and say, "Oh, wait, it's just a dream," and I go back to sleep, but we are still there. We run and run but don't make it. We try everything, but still no. I scream and scream each time she gets closer with horror. Oh no, she gets both of them! What am I going to do? Crying and shouting for help, they get closer and closer. But finally, I see light, and they are back! She's gone! What a relief... I wake up and say, "Phew... that's better."

Elena Uzunska (9)
St Mark's Primary School, Hanwell

There's A Spider In My Bed

There's a spider in my bed!
My feet started to wiggle
I tried to get out
But then my feet started to jiggle
It was Tinky Winky the spider
I hid in a cupboard as it scared me
Then I just realised
It was crawling on Dad's laundry
I tried to find the spider
It was hiding around
Then I saw
Some pants running like a hound
Dad to the rescue!
He really needed his pants
And with one swing of his axe
He killed the spider and got back his pants
Dad, you killed the spider
I shouted out loud
But it was annoying you and
On no! I ripped my dear, old pants
I was just playing a game and now my bed's full of sand
And I'm not happy as now I need a new bed.

Charlie Melville-Smith (9)
St Mark's Primary School, Hanwell

Sleep Paralysis

I woke up in a dream,
There was a sketchy monster
Standing in front of me,
I turned around and,
Started running, but I,
Didn't know where I was going.

I tried to shout *help!*
But no one was there,
I was so dead,
I ran and barged into,
A creepy house, I
Closed the door quickly,

I was gone from,
The monster, but where was I?
I looked around the house,
All I saw was a mouse,
I tried to wake up again,
That still didn't work.

I went downstairs again,
To look for clues,
But I saw the door,
Open, *creeaaakk!*

I looked behind me,
And there was the monster...
Heeelllppp!

Noah Sterritt (8)
St Mark's Primary School, Hanwell

Slide Suckers

We were going to a soft play,
We would have fun all day,
We went on the swings and roundabout,
Making us scream and shout.

We went down a slide, "Oh no!" said someone,
As the slide opened up,
Falling and falling into the darkness of night,
As we got close to the bottom, we could see a hint of light.

"Quick! The floor is lava!"
"Hop on any object before you die!"
We went object to object until we found the crown,
"You passed this time!" said someone we didn't know,
"Until you get past all the slides, you are stuck,
And you have one year until you die."

Toby Robinson (10)
St Mark's Primary School, Hanwell

Football Terror

I wake up to see,
A bunch of footballs around me.
The pitch is clear,
And night is near,
Scared for my life,
I might need a knife.
Hearing a frightening noise,
Crash, bang!
And the crowd goes wild,
Just like an angry crocodile.
Seeing the footballs line up to score,
I see a horde of dragons ready to roar.
I look in the audience and they look at me,
Realising live footballs are sipping their tea!
They light a huge campfire,
As it dances against the night sky,
While some of its sparks fly,
As quiet as a mouse they sneak up on me.

Nadia Timuri (10)
St Mark's Primary School, Hanwell

Are You Living Your Life?

There is a girl on your street,
As the full moon arrives,
She screams a question,
"Are you really living your life?"

She is pale and screams throughout the day,
As she sings on stage with her devil helper.
The girl shocks kids, but that's what she wants,
And at the end, she screams, *"Are you living your life?"*

She looks as scary as a green warlock,
And with a *bang* and a *crash*, she has arrived home.
Her home is full of dusty skulls,
Now she is home to get ready for the night...
To see if you are living your...?

Melissa Mills (9)
St Mark's Primary School, Hanwell

Candy Cane Land

In Candy Cane Land,
The houses are grand,
I look around, and my friend spots a person,
But instead of a person,
It's a mint humbug,
So then we lick it,
And we see a chicken,
Then I shout, "We're in Candy Cane Land!"
After that, we eat all the chocolate cars,
Not forgetting the Haribo bars,
But then I hear a rumble,
In an apple crumble,
So we run to our helicopter,
And watch the land,
Make a mountain,
But there is one problem,
We forgot to write a review on Tripadvisor,
Sorry, Candy Cane Land.

Hamish Tulleth (9)
St Mark's Primary School, Hanwell

Freaky Football

"Roar!" went the lion,
"Moo!" went the cow.
Entering the pitch,
Daydreaming about winning the crown.

"Kick-off," the animal army roared,
I leapt into action without a doubt.
Passing to my players in my defending zone,
I tackled and won the ball.

The further and further I went,
The more and more chance
I got at scoring a goal.
My heart soared as I scored.

The chocolate ball sat in the net,
As the keeper lowered his head in regret.

Rae Wells (10)
St Mark's Primary School, Hanwell

My Candy House

My house is made of candy,
A sweet delicious treat,
It's bright and bold,
Like a delicious treat,
My house is made of candy,
That you would want to eat.

My candy house is in a forest,
It's a lush, sweet treat,
My house is in a forest,
I'm sure you'd like to eat.

My forest is on a hill,
That's big and bold,
It's a tasty, green hill,
That's lovely and green,
The sun always shines and sings his lullaby.

Lottie Newton (7)
St Mark's Primary School, Hanwell

The Football Match

All I can see is football players scoring goals,
But the players have been given red and yellow cards,
Audiences cheering along,
There is nothing you can do,
Just scoring goals, is all the players can do.

Defenders defending the goals,
Goalkeepers saving the shots,
Strikers, striking in the box,
Left and right wing taking the throw-ins.

Winning the match,
Getting the Ballon d'Or,
Saving every goal,
Cheering with the crowd!

Yousef Mohammedi (7)
St Mark's Primary School, Hanwell

Rainy Day And Good Day

I'm sitting in a lonely house,
With nobody but a mouse,
Bang! Thud! Zap!

It's raining, I'm bored,
In every single way,
It's raining, I'm bored,
It's not going away,
Nobody in the street,
Nobody in the house,

Crash! Oh yay!
A ray of yellow sunshine,
Today is a good day.

This is my dream,
And I hope you have one, too,
Next time, I hope you have a good dream, too.

Ruby-May Howard (8)
St Mark's Primary School, Hanwell

Game And Candy Worlds

It's upside down in Dreamland,
I am in a game – a bright wonderful game.
I am with my best brother and my ginger cat.
I see a branch – a smooth branch,
I see a blue sky and a smooth floor.
I'm feeling happy as a happy emoji.
My brother is singing in the best tune he can,
My ginger cat smells cotton candy.
It tempts him to run away and get lost...
As the Earth spins back into its normal state,
My next adventure can't wait.

Livia Barros (7)
St Mark's Primary School, Hanwell

My Dream World

When I step into a purple portal
My sister grabs my hand
We slide down a huge pink slide
Into our dreamy wonderland
We look around (such sights to see!)
A whole new world just waiting for me
We see candy galore
Then we ride some unicorns!
We ride over a rainbow
We meet Barbie and Ken
And guess what, a hen!
We run back to a castle
Become princesses
Finally, we go back home
Phew, what a crazy day.

Isla-Mae Guy (8)
St Mark's Primary School, Hanwell

Lollipops And Rainbows

I wake up in a dreamland and look all around
Looking for things, what can be found?
Lollipops and rainbows and unicorns and bunnies
The scent of strawberries makes a rumble in my tummy
But then I bump into Ellie!
We laugh and joke and chit and chat
Then it starts to rain, *pit, pat, pat!*
When the rain stops
We hug each other goodbye
Thinking of what we could do when we come again next time.

Megha Mahesh (8)
St Mark's Primary School, Hanwell

Bunny World

I live in Bunny World,
Jumping all around.
I live in Bunny World,
Eating carrots on the ground.
I live in Bunny World,
Where lettuce is unbound.
I live in Bunny World,
Jumping like a hound.
I live in Bunny World,
Looking at carrot cake.
I live in Bunny World,
Where I bake.
I live in Bunny World,
With my bunny friend Jake.
I live in Bunny World,
Eating carrot cake.

Thomas Bartlett (9)
St Mark's Primary School, Hanwell

Will I Get There Some Day?

Clip-clop, noisy hooves,
Ears flopping, "Make him move!"
I bend forward,
Reins twisted,
Sky blue.
These are my wishes.
The sun smiles down,
The hooves touch the ground.
"But," to myself I say,
"Will I ever get there someday?"
But dreams aren't just dreams,
They're waving to the past.
So listen to your dreams,
Make your dreams last.

Dixie Weake (8)
St Mark's Primary School, Hanwell

Gojira

The wall surrounds me
Ready for its downfall
When we see Gojira
We start fighting
Gojira is a Titan
We have read
How not to be dead
When Gojira comes
Gojira gets his power from the sun
The sun is bright
None of this is right
As I escape through the stream
I realise it's all a dream
Until next time
Oh... breakfast time.

Rex Inns (8)
St Mark's Primary School, Hanwell

The Ocean

In the ocean
I see nothing in the ocean
I feel fine in the ocean
I'm with nobody in the ocean
A shark attack in the ocean
Nothing for miles in the ocean
I get bored in the ocean
I get splashed in the ocean
Finally, land beside the ocean
I get home from the ocean
This is fine and the ocean is nice
All from a tiny island in the ocean.

Adam Bessaih (7)
St Mark's Primary School, Hanwell

The Dark World

It was just a normal day,
Nothing new,
When I fell through a trapdoor,
And my mind blew.

I was in a forest,
With nothing to see.
Then came a devil and demon,
Trying to kill me!

I felt horrified as they chased me,
Into a Minecraft world.
The warden and a creeper found me,
And all the earth swirled.

Stanley Goodwin (8)
St Mark's Primary School, Hanwell

Pegasus Field

In Pegasus Field, the grass is as green as an emerald,
The sky is as clear as water,
The clouds are a light, creamy pink,
Me and Sofia are linked,
Like BFFs and so in sync,
I think it's time to say,
Goodbye to Pegasus Field,
And all the Pegasuses that live there.

Jessica Hardy (8)
St Mark's Primary School, Hanwell

My Mythical World

Above me fly dragons high
Soaring up in the sky
Below me Zim, by my side
She is my special guide
All around me, creatures run
They all are having so much fun!
Millions of experiences all in one
I wish to do this every day
But I have school anyway.

Stella Davey (9)
St Mark's Primary School, Hanwell

Underwater Castle

It is nice and cool down here,
The dolphins jump and play.
I hear the splashing of the dolphins,
And the spraying of the whales.
The shells feel cold and smooth,
My mum takes me into my underwater bed,
And then says goodnight.

Ellie Hlinican (8)
St Mark's Primary School, Hanwell

Rainbow Skittle Land

In my dreams, rainbows taste like Skittles
However, the green Skittles taste like pickles
As I slowly walk outside falling Skittles all fall on me
Above my head I see marshmallows shaped like bees

The fluffy white clouds are like cotton candy
It's quite funny as the ocean tastes like shandy
There are sherbert yellow sunflowers that are so tall
But it looks so strange as the trees are so small!

The red Skittles look like a ball
Watch out, get the green pickle Skittles as they fall!
The clouds are shaped like hearts
And they taste like tarts

As I walk among the floor
There are more and more!
Everywhere is the colour of a rainbow
It's as bright and colourful as a West End show!

Mia Watkin (8)
St Mary's CE Primary School, Barnsley

If We Could Fly

The sky is as blue as the ocean,
The sun is as bright as an explosion,
In my dreams, I can fly,
It is so cool, I am so up high.

My hair is blowing in the wind,
I can't help but sing,
My arms are stretched out wide,
As I twirl and glide.

I got to go to Australia,
I like to play at Playmania,
I got to stay up all night,
I need to turn on the light.

I finally fly home,
But I realise I am all alone,
I find a BFF for me,
I say to her, "My name is Feefee."

I feel as free as a bird!
As I swoop and swirl,
I am a really lucky girl!

I fly up the mountains,
Touching the sky,
The volcano is so hot,
I must be careful not to die.

Sophia Cassell (9)
St Mary's CE Primary School, Barnsley

Waking Up In New York

In my dream, I woke up in New York
I wanted food but I needed a fork
I wanted some nuts
But the shop was shut!

I went for a long walk
But I only saw a hawk
I went on a boat ride
I saw the Statue of Liberty
At the boat side!

I went to a party
Where I ate a Smartie
I came back at midnight
And I went to the hotel to sleep tight

I skated in Central Park
The lights were twinkling as it was almost dark
Tiffany's window sparkled in the night
It was such a wonderful sight!

I travelled to Barnsley
Where I'm from
I don't know how I got here all along
I went home to my room
So I could watch Tutankhamun.

Georgia Rose Peace (8)
St Mary's CE Primary School, Barnsley

Raining Money

In my dream, the world rains money,
After I got some money, I went to buy some honey,
The honey was as sticky as melted chocolate,
However, there was some money on a bunny

I nearly had ten thousand pounds,
All from spinning around,
I felt like a new king,
It was better because the season was spring.

I woke up and opened the window, and money filled my bed,
Suddenly, some money hit me on the head.
There was that much I could not blink,
Suddenly, the money turned pink.

I went to the shop and everyone had loads of things,
However, I only had some strings,
With my string, I made a skipping rope,
Only with a bit of hope!

Teddy Cassell (8)
St Mary's CE Primary School, Barnsley

Football Land

In my dreams, footballers looked like giant footballs
It was hard to play any games
And all they seemed to do was hit all the walls
You couldn't play, which seemed a shame.

When the ball zoomed into the net
The crowd would clap and cheer
They were all happy to win their bets
As they all celebrated with beer.

Barnsley, player eleven, dribbled into the net
Someone scored with pleasure
Someone shouted and screamed, hoping they would win
They would never lose, ever.

Distant shirts dashed about
Full of skill, there's no doubt
They were so clever and ran so fast
As I called, they ran past.

Gracie Gibbons (9)
St Mary's CE Primary School, Barnsley

Water Land

In my dream, the world is made of water,
It's so beautiful it makes me want to be an author.
Everywhere is dark blue,
I cannot believe the beautiful view!

Everywhere we have to swim,
It's like going to the gym.
No one drives any cars,
They drive around in boats like superstars.

I spend lots of time on a float,
Trying not to gloat.
I spend lots of time drinking Coca-Cola,
And I love to eat lots of granola!

There are lots of bright and exotic fish,
One of them can help you make a wish.
The world is wonderful and sparkly,
It's better than working at Barclays!

Elva Clegg (9)
St Mary's CE Primary School, Barnsley

My Friendly Dragon

In my dream, I dream of a dragon,
I found him in my dad's wagon!
I gave him a slice of meat and tamed him,
I think I should give him a name and call him Jim!

I taught him to do some tricks,
Something like a mid-air backflip!
Now he learnt how to hunt fish,
It is now my next dish!

At night when I entered his cave,
I saw him trying to sunbathe!
This was such a funny sight,
Luckily I got my night light!

When we were playing, he roared in my face,
My ears felt like they were hit by a mace!
We would play all day,
We never got tired of play!

Sherry Liang (9)
St Mary's CE Primary School, Barnsley

Dragon Land

In my dreams, there was a land of dragons,
I don't know how this had happened,
There was a dragon that was boring,
He slept all day, and I was fed up with all his snoring.

In Dragon Land, there was a lot of poo,
It looked like a river as it was blue,
The food at Dragon Land tasted so bad,
I was so hungry it made me mad.

There was a dragon that was bad,
It made the other dragons sad,
A dragon had a look,
Then he ripped a book.

All the dragons went to bed,
So I read,
In the morning, I baked a cake,
It took a long time to make.

Georgia Skidmore (9)
St Mary's CE Primary School, Barnsley

I Can Eat Everything

My pillow tastes like cotton candy,
I got it from my lovely daddy,
I went to my dad to ask for a snack,
He said, "Yes, get it out of the candy sack!"

I got some Smarties,
They tasted nasty,
I got a drink; it was pink,
I took a sip - it tasted like ink!
I took a bite out of a tree,
Pop! It was quite a minty treat!
Next, I went to the flower bed,
I ate the flowers; the best flavour was red!

Just before it was time for sleep,
I ate a bee; it tasted like meat!
Now, my tummy is all full
Because I have had a bagful!

Emily Hodgkinson (9)
St Mary's CE Primary School, Barnsley

I Have 1,000 Cats

In my dream, cats were like rugs
But unfortunately, some had bugs!
Some cats had magical powers,
They got their powers from eating flowers!

I divided them into groups of forty
Then named one cat Morty.
He howled and growled,
He sounded like he was being drowned!

The cats stayed there for hours
And I started eating flowers!
They looked like sleeping mud,
Then suddenly, they woke up!

They trotted home like a train,
Their fluff was like a mane.
When we got home, I gave them fish,
Then outside came the mist!

India Ibbeson (8)
St Mary's CE Primary School, Barnsley

Time Travel

The lollipops were so sweet,
All the chicks tweeted at our feet,
My dream world was made of candy,
It could be very handy!

Next, I flew to Japan,
A drunk man hit me with a frying pan,
So I fought back
I hit him with a full black sack.

After that, I got the power to turn into a T-rex,
In the ocean, in the distance, I saw a shipwreck,
I found an abandoned army camp,
I had to turn on a lamp.

I found a portal to the Stone Age,
Sadly, I got trapped in a cage,
After a while, I broke out,
In joy, I ran about.

Tobias Sekanina (9)
St Mary's CE Primary School, Barnsley

Candyland

In my dream, the world was made out of candy.
I thought this was quite handy.
The candy was so sweet,
I was too excited, such a treat.

The clouds tasted like candyfloss,
Then Mr Candyman was very cross.
I ate the marshmallows, my mouth went crazy.
There was a gingerbread man named Davy.

I felt so happy,
I felt like I could pop!
I ate more sweets,
I couldn't stop.

The red gummy bear tasted like strawberries,
The pink gummies tasted like raspberries.
The chocolate was yummy,
It was all in my tummy.

Amarachi Eze (8)
St Mary's CE Primary School, Barnsley

Raining Animals

In my world, raining animals were great,
Something I think no one would hate,
I got a beautiful free pet dog,
He loved to play and hop with all the frogs.

I got ready to explore,
I knew there had to be so much more,
The lion gave out a mega *roar!*
All while the rabbits gave out a snore.

As the donkey led the way,
It gave out a massive *neigh!*
I went home with a smile
Although it took a while.

As I got ready to lie down,
I suddenly made an upside-down frown,
The last thing I heard that was *moo!*
The first thing I heard the next morning was *cockadoodledoo!*

Zach Morgan (8)
St Mary's CE Primary School, Barnsley

Candy Land

In my dreams, this place is made of candy,
Sometimes, it can be quite handy.
I live on a street,
Which always has plenty of treats.

I feel really jolly,
And my name is Holly.
Everywhere is fun and sweet,
I think I live on the best street!

In the street, the trees are cotton candy,
Yum! Delicious! Fine and dandy!
You can eat the streets while you walk,
Enjoy it with friends while you talk.

The sweets shrank me,
I was scared, so I hid behind a tree,
I suddenly woke,
It was a dream and a joke!

Vanesa Jokimciute (9)
St Mary's CE Primary School, Barnsley

Back In Time!

I woke up in a tent,
It looked slightly bent.
The wolves' eyes glowed in the dark,
It stood out from the bark!

I went down to the river,
It made me quiver.
I stabbed my spear in the river for fish,
They went on a dish.

Zoom! The spear flew through the air,
Nobody seemed to care.
Cave paintings on the wall,
Everyone seemed so small.

This was a weird world,
And at night, while everyone was curled,
I thought, *they've crossed the battle line*,
I'd gone back in time!

Jack Thornton (9)
St Mary's CE Primary School, Barnsley

Controlling Everything

In my dream, I could control everything.
Everything was as light as a piece of string.
People were so afraid.
Then they thought I would start a raid!

I lifted a tree easily from the ground.
Then I saw a rabbit bound.
I held it up with a finger.
People did not linger.

I went home with a smile.
Then I ran one mile.
And I saw a crocodile.
So, I named him Kyle.

I threw a car; it landed with a crash!
And it made a building smash.
A car stampeded like a bull.
Then, I made the engine pull.

Theo Gaskell-Booth (9)
St Mary's CE Primary School, Barnsley

Japan

I woke up in fascinating Japan!
Some bandits came, so I defended myself with a frying pan
My frying pan bonked them on the heads
They all acted as if they were dead!

I went to the city to buy some memories from my occasional trip
On the way, I did a little skip, good job I didn't trip!
I wanted to learn Japanese
I did it with such ease

On the way home, I saw where I woke up
I was thirsty, so a waiter gave me water and a cup
It was an enjoyable time
I will be looking forward to another time!

Borys Patyk (9)
St Mary's CE Primary School, Barnsley

I Adopted All The Animals In The World, Even Dragons And Unicorns!

In my dreams there were dragons,
It was quite funny as they were driving wagons!
There were some unicorns in the night,
It was such a marvellous sight!

The unicorns were sparkly pink,
It made me stop and think,
If unicorns were my pet,
I wondered if they would need a vet!

There was a dragon called Toothless,
He was useless!
There were two twins,
They always fight,
In the black of the night!

There were dragons,
Who were always eating candy on wagons!

Rose Karimi (9)
St Mary's CE Primary School, Barnsley

Candyland

The fluffy clouds are like cotton candy
I think they might come in handy
They were so bright it made me blink!
They were my favourite colour - pink!

I could see lollies as big as a house
There were mint trees as small as a mouse
Jellybeans so squishy and red
They reminded me of a soft, cosy bed

There was ice cream yellow and cold
I needed to have a hold
It looked so tasty and smelled so yummy
Could I have a taste? It needs to be in my tummy!

Lailah Braithwaite (9)
St Mary's CE Primary School, Barnsley

Ice World

In my dream, the world was made of ice,
I was a princess and I looked so nice,
I had a special power,
I wanted a friend,
But it had to end.

I ate some ice cream,
But I heard someone scream,
She had a twin called Milly,
But we decided to play dab,
But I wish it was Rome,
I had to say goodbye,
I had the time of my life.

Johana Jintu (8)
St Mary's CE Primary School, Barnsley

My Weird Family

There are a lot of families, such as fancy families, swanky families and dirty, stinky and manky families. But I have the weirdest of families and here it goes...
My brother: My brother is seven years old and he had a house, but now it has been sold (never too young and never too old).
Now, my sister: My sister is thirteen years old and she's more like an infected blister than a sister. She's so mucky and old, she's always getting told.
Now, my mum: My mum is so loud, she should be a drum.
Oh no, my dad: When you meet my dad, you should be sad; he farts like mad and they smell so bad!
But the weirdest thing in my family is me.
I woke up, and thankfully, it was just a dream.

Sienna-Marie Roberts (10)
St Thomas CE (VC) Primary School, Bradley

All About Dancers And Their Moves

A long time ago there were five dancers called, Lily, Grace, Emma, Emily and Summer, their dance teacher was called Mayah. The dancers had a big secret... They were... fairies!

At the end of every lesson, Summer would get changed and put on her wings and be the beautiful fairy she was. Once the girls had finished their lesson and returned to their fairy world, they would put on a show, and Summer would tell everyone to come to see their new moves. The way the girls danced was amazing, they would twirl and spin and twirl some more. But one day they were all locked up and the fairies were no more.

Dae'naja Bedeau (10)
St Thomas CE (VC) Primary School, Bradley

Football

He is running up the pitch like he is doing a width
The player is marking
The player is laughing
The person is walking
Someone is drawing
Skills over the hills
Travelling miles in the wild
Who is dribbling
I am writing
The doorbell is ringing
My team is winning
Through the Premier
A good grin
With the win.

Joshua Norman-Mcleoud (10)
St Thomas CE (VC) Primary School, Bradley

Spring Allotment

Down in my allotment
Plants shoot up to the sky
Growing taller and taller every day
Valuable vegetables if we try

As leaves grow and thrive
All my precious veg grows
Nice and juicy
Whilst my girlfriend mows

Whilst it's warm
I make some shade
I'm in my shed
Which is man-made.

Josh Stead (10)
St Thomas CE (VC) Primary School, Bradley

Fear Breaking

Erin, Adele and Belle sleeping soundly,
All was fine until they woke up in some dream
They were in a room of spiders.
Adele screamed, waving her hands up and down
Erin and Belle guided Adele to a corner, leaning back
Erin whispered things to Adele trying to help calm her down
While Belle trampled on the spiders.
Adele whispered, "I do not fear this!"
The walls disappeared, suddenly plummeting them down.
They walked down a corridor thin as could be,
Walking into a room full of disappointed faces facing Erin
This was Erin's fear, disappointing people
Terrifying for her
She walked through the room, scared to see the faces
Terrified to see their thoughts
They felt a door handle, twisting it fast.
They all entered the room they were sleeping in.
They all fell on the sleeping bags and went back to sleep
Just to wake up in the third room on top of a building.

Lowri Thomas (11)
Tavernspite Community Primary School, Whitland

My Bright And Beautiful Dream Garden

In my dream garden,
A bright and beautiful garden,
I feel calm and joyful,
As I walk between the blossoming cherry trees,
Their light pink flowers, swaying in the breeze,
Their branches are weighed down by the blooms and the lush green leaves.

It is spring in my garden,
The bold bluebells have made magical carpets,
The blackbirds are making their nests again,
In the dense conifers and leafy hedges,
The blue tits are darting cheerfully around the willows,
And the vibrant daffodils and cowslips nod their delicate heads,
As the playful rabbits happily hop by.

It is summer in my garden,
The sweet apples are finally ripe,
The purple lavender is now in bloom,
The bees are buzzing and the butterflies are fluttering,
The bright and warm sunlight sparkles on the clear water of the stream,

And in the evening, when the sun sinks below the horizon,
The streaks of pink and orange across the sky promise a lovely new day ahead.

It is autumn in my garden,
The leaves have turned orange and red, and have floated down to the floor,
The wind now blows hard and fierce, picking up the leaves and making them perform a swirling dance.
Though the more gloomy weather has returned, the sun still glows through the raindrops.
And during the later hours of the day, the bats swirl and flap,
Their performance really is an amazing sight to see.

It is winter in my garden,
Most of the trees are now bare.
Though the holly berries have now grown,
And the conifers still have their needles,
The air is getting more chilly,
And the bird baths get covered by thick sheets of ice,
The snow in the garden does not come often,
But the frosted plants twinkle in the sunrise.

My dream garden is full of wildlife.
In the wooded areas, there are fox cubs in the spring,
They leap and bounce playfully in the early morning light.
In the night, the badgers and the owls come out.
There are sometimes even deer in the evenings.
There are squirrels and rabbits too, and lots of birds.
Finches, tits, warblers, I love to watch them all.
Buzzards and red kites fly high above me, gliding gracefully,
There's also, of course, the bees, the butterflies, the beetles and spiders,
Seeing them all is a real treat!

I really do love my bright and beautiful dream garden,
I would love to walk round the paths, or climb the trees, or relax in the sunlight, reading a good book.
Although my dream garden is just a part of my imagination,
One day, could I have a garden like this of my own?

Mischa Orford (11)
Tavernspite Community Primary School, Whitland

Space Journey

S eparations are the best things about rockets, it's like a puzzle.
P lanet Mars, we go next.
A round and around as we orbit.
C ircles a barrel roll, but hope we don't flip.
E ternal space as it goes on.

J erking and jerking as the ride goes on.
O ne day, we might get there.
U ntil then we will be
R acing and racing against time.
N o way it's going to beat us.
E ntering Mars as we burn up.
Y ou and me, watching the sun go down.

Spencer Reynolds (11)
Tavernspite Community Primary School, Whitland

The Magical Island

In a land of dreams
Where fantasies come to play
A magical island awaits
Just a boat ride away
With emerald seas and
Golden sands so fine
This enchanting paradise
Is truly divine.

The air is filled with
Whispers of ancient lore
As mermaids sing and
Seashells gently explore
Fairies dance upon
The petals of blooming flowers
While unicorns graze
In enchanted bowers.

Tropical birds paint the sky
With vibrant hues
As palm trees sway
To the rhythm
Of the ocean's muse
Waiting to be discovered
By the brave and bold.

Pippa Thomas (11)
Tavernspite Community Primary School, Whitland

Secrets Of The 'Big Bad Wolf'

In the woods so deep and wide,
I found myself taken for a wild ride,
Wolves surrounded me, big and strong,
But their hearts were gentle all along.

They whisked me away, through trees we dashed,
Their paws so soft, their eyes so kind and flashed,
No fear of harm, just playful delight,
We became friends under the moon's light.

In the wolf pack, I found my place,
Running free in nature's embrace,
No longer kidnapped but part of their crew,
With friendly wolves, my heart found something true.

Jack Leyfield (11)
Tavernspite Community Primary School, Whitland

The Christmas Terror

Mind full of presents
And goodies, you sleep
Suddenly, you hear a *thud* beneath your feet
"Santa!" you cry as you run down the stairs
Although the sight you see stands up all your hairs
Santa has bright red eyes
Long claws
And sharp teeth
He hands you a stocking, and your legs feel like lead
He goes into the garden to fetch the sled
The stocking, you find, is full of hay
You frown and think, *this has been a very odd day!*

Cedi Michael (11)
Tavernspite Community Primary School, Whitland

Fishing

F ar, far away, in a land of beasts
I n the land, although there were beasts, they had some great fishing spots
S ome of the fish were so big you could see them from a mile away
H ow - you're probably thinking about how massive they were
I n the land, there were majestic fish. They were almost as beautiful as the best flower
N ancy was the biggest fish ever
G lory, just catching one of these.

Harri H
Tavernspite Community Primary School, Whitland

Jurassic

J ourneying to other time and place
U nbelievable sights I witness, amazement on my face
R eal dinosaurs roam freely, humbly, proudly
A round me these giants march, my heart's racing
S ights and smells of the Jurassic era
S teadily a diplodocus wanders closer
I hold my breath and reach out my hand
C almly the creature welcomes me to his land.

Matty May (10)
Tavernspite Community Primary School, Whitland

Bedtime

B ridge with a wolf on it
E erie only a little bit
D ead of night
T ables turn as the wolf bites
I nvestigators find the body
M illions find out
E nchanted Forest was the last time I was around.

Elsie Fowler (11)
Tavernspite Community Primary School, Whitland

She Comes At Night

As night-time came, I lay in bed
Thoughts of my day filling my head
I closed my eyes and shut them tight
I heard my parents say goodnight

I tossed and turned, head in a whirl
Then saw something glistening, like a small girl
A tiny dark shadow with very pointed feet
Swaying to the rhythm, dancing to the beat

My alarm went off, I sat up in my bed
Did I just make all this up in my head?
I spent the day thinking a lot
Was it a dream or was it not?

In my bed that night she came again
Swirling and whirling and prancing and then
My alarm sounded and I jumped out of bed
I couldn't stop thinking who that was in my head

The day raced by, I was ready to sleep
I shut my eyes, didn't make a peep
I wondered and wondered who it could be...
I finally realised... she was me!

Erin Simkins (9)
Two Gates Community Primary School, Two Gates

Be Kind

It doesn't matter if someone is small,
We should always be kind to them.
It doesn't matter if someone is tall,
We should always be kind to them.
It doesn't matter if someone wears glasses,
We should always be kind to them.
It doesn't matter what colour someone's hair is,
We should always be kind to them.
I dream, in the future, everyone will be kind
And no one will call me small.
Everyone is different and that's okay,
So don't be mean to them.
We should always be kind to them.

Georgie-May Haynes (10)
Two Gates Community Primary School, Two Gates

When I Make The Team

When I make the team,
I will be a shooting star.

When I make the team,
I will hear the crowds roar my name.

When I make the team,
I will never back down.

When I make the team,
I will lead my team to glory.

When I make the team,
I will make my country proud.

When I make the team,
Nothing will stop me.

Olivia May Kidd (9)
Two Gates Community Primary School, Two Gates

Super Dream

I'm in a dream
I see a beam,
What should I do except scream?

I see heroes,
I see an arrow,
I ask them and they say it's a shadow.

I say hi,
The villain says, "Die!"
And he picks up his two scythes.

Then we fly,
And they cry,
We called them too shy.

Rayyan Chaudhry (10)
Two Gates Community Primary School, Two Gates

My Life

Once there was a girl, who longed for a pearl,
She had a cat and a pet bat,
Her hat sat stuck on the mat,
The cat doesn't attack the bat on his back.
She does not think about stuff which links,
She collects all the ink to use for her work.
And stuff that lurks
She is very boring and her dad is snoring,
She has a tank that looks like a bank,
Because of her money, she is the sweetest honey.
Her cat always tugs over loads of bugs,
And spills over rugs, coffee in mugs.
The cat sees a dog and wants to hog,
She jumps over a log, skims past a frog,
All in the fog.
My favourite boy has a nice toy.
I put on a bow and crouch down low,
With my light shining bright,
This is my life.
It cuts like a knife,
But I like it.

Siya Samani (8)
Whitchurch Primary School & Nursery, Stanmore

I Have A Dream!

Yesterday, a wonderful secret I uncovered,
That there's a magnificent land, waiting to be discovered.
It's a place beyond the stars,
Where there's beauty and there are scars.
It's a place where friendships blossom,
And living there is *genuinely* awesome.
Magic lives in the clouds and the sky,
And if you're smart, you're not gonna lie.
'Cause the Sorting Hat knows everyone's fate,
And you better not put up a debate.
There are magical creatures and sweets that make you feel funny,
Also, there's a boy named Ron who loves to say, 'bloody'!

In the unknown walls of this mysterious castle,
Lies an array of excitement, chaos and lots of challenges to tackle.
But fights the golden trio with all their might,
Till *You-Know-Who* is out of sight.

Romance lives in the air,
And Christmas is a great time to show that you care.
'Cause as the mystical snow touches your heart,
Maybe it can help create a spark.

Just remember to stick with your friends no matter how fast the situation gets scary,
Like how Hermione, Ron and Ginny stuck with Harry.

I have a dream to live in a place filled with wizards and witches,
And spells and Quidditch.
A place where people aren't fake,
I keep asking myself, do I have what it takes?

I have a dream to go to a place,
Where no one will betray,
I have a dream to go to Hogwarts *one day*...

Trisha Bhatnagar (11)
Whitchurch Primary School & Nursery, Stanmore

My Dragons

My dragons fly.
Very, very high.
I feel the winds.
I see grey tints.

My dragons' scales on their wings,
are ever so comfortable.
My dragons' scales on their wings,
are ever so unforgettable.

I feel so joyful.
My dragons are so playful.
I am so careful.
My dragons are so playful.

I like my dreams.
It is how it seems.
My dreams,
My dragon dreams.

My dragon of light,
has colours which are so bright.
Its power is at a great height.
It's my dragon of light.

My dragon of dark,
has colours of the night.
Its power is at a great height.
It's my dragon of dark.

My dragons form a robot knight, when they are in trouble.
The robot knight is indestructible.
It has the power of light.
It has the power of dark.

My dragons protect their land.
My dragons are my henchmen.
Now that's all for my dragon dreams.

Shrien Varsani (10)
Whitchurch Primary School & Nursery, Stanmore

I Closed My Eyes And I Could See...

I closed my eyes and I could see the homework that I'd left open. Then I went to bed until *bang! Boom!* Oh! Oh! It was something nearby but I don't know. I woke up. I had to go to my dance class. I met a new dancer. My teacher said I should always be good if someone was new in the class. The headteachers came with a writer. *Boom!* I heard that sound again. I felt like I was somewhere like a... workshop. I realised that there was something moving in the shadows. *I think... I think I see it. Oh! I think it's an invisible clown. No, it's an invisible wizard!* It had spiders in a jar and it had fairies in a jar, but suddenly, I got a fright. I woke up and I saw home sweet home.

Sefora Matis Bumb (9)
Whitchurch Primary School & Nursery, Stanmore

Mystical World

M agic sprinkling everywhere you look,
Y et nothing will stop the sparkles twinkling,
S pells and unicorns faced everywhere,
T all castles towering high in its beauty,
I t has the blossomed flowers scared of daylight,
C astles with life filled around them,
A ll of it makes you charmed,
L ove spreads across every step you take.

W herever you go, beauty is here,
O h, the fairies gleaming with brightness,
R aindrops fall,
L ovely roses bloom,
D oes anything feel better than having a mystical world?

Reeva Rabadiya (9)
Whitchurch Primary School & Nursery, Stanmore

Let's Go To Wembley To Win A Chicken Dinner

You're in Wembley to score the winner,
So you can win a chicken dinner,
If you don't,
You won't,
So you better,
Or you will never,
If you want to meet Messi,
You first have to get Pepsi,
Because your room is messy,
While eating cream,
Because this was all a dream.

Hriday Patel (9)
Whitchurch Primary School & Nursery, Stanmore

A Star In The Sky

A star in the sky,
Leading the pathway
Of my
Destiny!

A star in the sky,
Even brighter than
The light in my
Bright eyes!

This light in the sky
Fills the whole world with love,
And dreams of which
Can make a world a world again!

Anahi Lily Gandhi-Mehta (9)
Whitchurch Primary School & Nursery, Stanmore

Dream

My dream is to be
in the police, the army
or a teacher.
This is my dream, not like others.

Prince Patel (10)
Whitchurch Primary School & Nursery, Stanmore

I Love Winter

I love winter and here is why,
Even though there's mostly grey in the sky.
I love winter, the sun's not so strong,
So I don't have to put greasy suncream on.
I love winter, the grass covered in white,
Reflecting the moonlight on a clear night.
I love winter and building people with snow,
Even though it warms up, they'll go.
I love winter when Christmas time comes,
And our seats are filled with my family's bums.
I love winter, snuggled up by the fire,
The crackling flames make my spirit higher.
I love winter, movie nights with Mummy,
With popcorn and marshmallows filling my tummy.
I love winter and that was why,
Even though there's mostly grey in the sky.

Jessica Naylor (8)
White Notley CE (VC) Primary School, White Notley

A Magical World

I was flying so fast, soaring through the sky.
I saw colours of all different kinds, I caught a glimpse of clouds full of happy thoughts.
Wonderful creatures with magic untold.

The sun was shining so brightly with a tune of its own.
Amazing things I've never seen before.

The more I explored, the more joy came to my heart.
And in that very moment, I knew I never wanted to awaken.

In that world, I was free, imagination flowing through me.
"Anything is possible," I screamed in my head.
As creatures of all kinds sang and flew, as I let myself go.

Isabella Sapienza (8)
White Notley CE (VC) Primary School, White Notley

Greetings From Fairyland

I sat in my bed, ready to sleep
I did not hear a single peep
I closed my eyes
And to my surprise
I dreamed about me
And a wonderful tree
About a fairy
Who loved to eat dairy
Who had a friend
Who was a little bit hairy
About a unicorn
Who cut her hoof on a thorn
Who loved to jump
On a pillow of Flumps
We danced with no fear
Before they all disappeared
What a wonderful night it had been.

Amaia Franklin (8)
White Notley CE (VC) Primary School, White Notley

Just A Dream

I look to my left,
I look to my right,
Nothing.
So I get quite a fright.
I look up and,
I look down,
Nothing.
So I just turn around.
What is this feeling
Of the walls closing in?
It's like they are sharp,
As a shark's fin.
Then I wake up and start to scream,
Then I remember,
It's just a dream.

Maya Kassan-Lawrence (9)
White Notley CE (VC) Primary School, White Notley

YoungWriters
Est. 1991

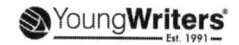

YOUNG WRITERS INFORMATION

We hope you have enjoyed reading this book – and that you will continue to in the coming years.

If you're a young writer who enjoys reading and creative writing, or the parent of an enthusiastic poet or story writer, do visit our website **www.youngwriters.co.uk**. Here you will find free competitions, workshops and games, as well as recommended reads, a poetry glossary and our blog.

If you would like to order further copies of this book, or any of our other titles, then please give us a call or visit **www.youngwriters.co.uk**.

Young Writers
Remus House
Coltsfoot Drive
Peterborough
PE2 9BF
(01733) 890066
info@youngwriters.co.uk

- YoungWritersUK
- YoungWritersCW
- youngwriterscw
- youngwriterscw